The Humpty Dumpty Book

Illustrated by
Jean Chandler

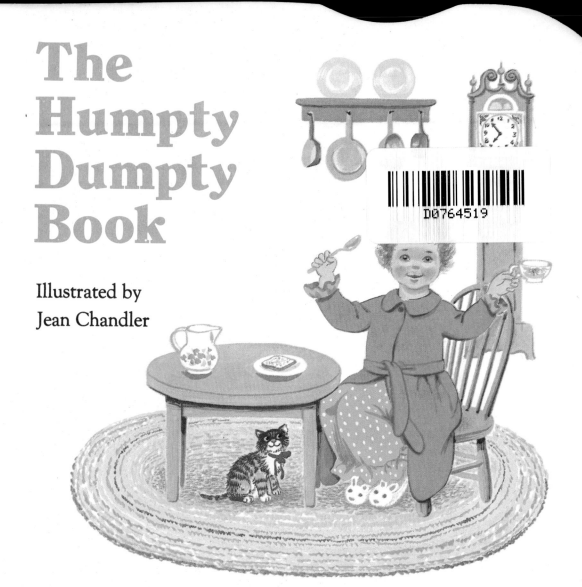

A GOLDEN BOOK · NEW YORK

Western Publishing Company, Inc., Racine, Wisconsin 53404

B C D E F G H I J

Humpty Dumpty

Humpty Dumpty sat on a wall,
Humpty Dumpty had a great fall,
All the King's horses and all the King's men
Couldn't put Humpty together again.

Get Up, Get Up

A birdie with a yellow bill
Hopped upon my windowsill,
Cocked his shining eye and said,
"Get up, get up, you sleepyhead!"

Sippity Sup,
Sippity Sup

Sippity sup, sippity sup,
Bread and milk from a china cup,
Bread and milk from a bright silver spoon,
Made of a piece of the bright silver moon!
Sippity sup, sippity sup,
Sippity, sippity sup!

The Muffin Man

O do you know the muffin man,
The muffin man, the muffin man,
O do you know the muffin man
That lives in Drury Lane?

O yes, I know the muffin man,
The muffin man, the muffin man,
O yes, I know the muffin man
That lives in Drury Lane.

123

1 for the money
2 for the show
3 to make ready
And 4 to go!

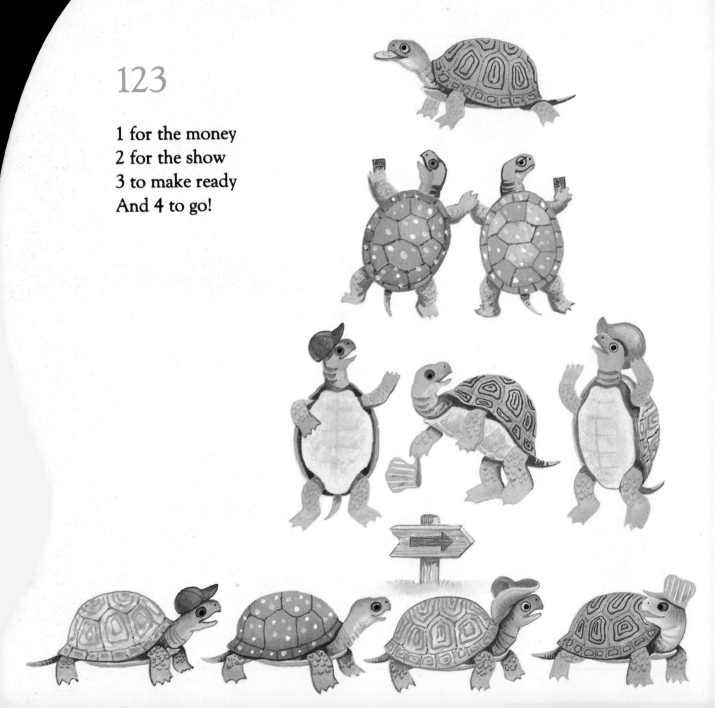

ABC

ABC, tumbledown D,
The cat's in the cupboard
And can't see me.

Little Betty Blue

Little Betty Blue
Lost her holiday shoe,
What can little Betty do?
Give her another
To match the other,
And then she may walk in two.

Handy Pandy

Handy Pandy, Jack-a-dandy,
Loves plum cake and sugar candy.
He bought some at a grocer's shop,
And out he came, hop, hop, hop!

To Market, To Market

To market, to market, to buy a fat pig,
Home again, home again, jiggety jig.
To market, to market, to buy a fat hog,
Home again, home again, jiggety jog.

Dickory, Dickory, Dare

Dickory, dickory, dare,
The pig flew up in the air,
The man in brown soon brought him down,
Dickory, dickory, dare.

Simple Simon

Simple Simon met a pieman, going to the fair,
Says Simple Simon to the pieman, "Let me taste your ware."
Says the pieman to Simple Simon, "Show me first your penny."
Says Simple Simon to the pieman, "Indeed I have not any."

Peter Piper

Peter Piper picked a peck of pickled peppers,
A peck of pickled peppers Peter Piper picked.
If Peter Piper picked a peck of pickled peppers,
Where's the peck of pickled peppers Peter Piper picked?

My Little Hen

I had a little hen, the prettiest ever seen,
She washed me the dishes and kept the house clean,
She went to the mill to fetch me some flour,
She brought it home in less than an hour,
She baked me my bread, she brewed me my ale,
She sat by the fire and told many a fine tale.

Three Little Mice

Three Little Mice sat down to spin,
Pussy passed by and she peeped in.
"Shall I come in and bite off your threads?"
"Oh, no, Miss Pussy, you'd snip off our heads."
"No, I'll not—I'll help you spin."
"That may be so, but you can't come in!"

The Cat and
the Fiddle

Hey, diddle, diddle!
The cat and the fiddle,
The cow jumped over the moon;
The little dog laughed to see such sport,
And the dish ran away with the spoon.

Come to the Window

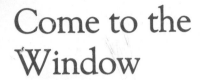

Come to the window,
My baby, with me,
And look at the stars
That shine on the sea!
There are two little stars
That play at bo-peep
With two little fish
Far down in the deep;
And two little frogs
Cry neap, neap, neap;
I see a dear baby
That should be asleep.

The Little Maid

There was a little maid
And she had a light guitar,
And when the moon was bright,
She sang tra, la, tra, la.

Jack, Be Nimble

Jack, be nimble,
Jack, be quick,
Jack, jump over the candlestick.